Today Was a Terrible Day

Today Was a Terrible Day

by Patricia Reilly Giff

illustrated by Susanna Natti

Puffin Books

PUFFIN BOOKS

A Division of Penguin Books USA Inc.
375 Hudson Street, New York, New York 10014
Penguin Books Ltd, 27 Wrights Lane, London W8 5TZ England
Penguin Books Australia Ltd, Ringwood, Victoria, Australia
Penguin Books Canada Ltd, 10 Alcorn Avenue, Toronto, Ontario, Canada M4V 3B2
Penguin Books (N.Z.) Ltd, 182-190 Wairau Road, Auckland 10, New Zealand

Penguin Books Ltd, Registered Offices: Harmondsworth, Middlesex, England

First published in 1980 by The Viking Press 1982
Published in Picture Puffins 1984

11   13   15   17   19   20   18   16   14   12

Text copyright © 1980 by Patricia Reilly Giff
Illustrations copyright © 1980 by Susanna Natti
All rights reserved

Library of Congress Cataloging in Publication Data
Giff, Patricia Reilly.   Today was a terrible day.
Summary: Follows the humorous mishaps of a second
grader who is learning to read.
[1. Reading—Fiction.]   I. Natti, Susanna, ill.   II. Title.
PZ7.G3626To   1984   [E]   83-24482   ISBN 0-14-050453-2

Manufactured in the U.S.A.

For my sons, Jim and Bill
P.R.G.

For my parents
S.N.

Today was a terrible day.

It started when I dropped my pencil.

Miss Tyler asked, "Ronald Morgan,

why are you crawling under the

table like a snake?"

Now all the children call me Snakey.

When Miss Tyler told us to take out
last night's homework, I noticed that
my mother had forgotten to sign mine.
I quickly signed it for her
so she wouldn't get in trouble.
But Miss Tyler said, "Ronald Morgan.
It is a crime to sign other people's names.
And you spelled your mother's name wrong."
All the children laughed.

Later, when Billy was reading
—he's in the Satellite group—
I got hungry, and my stomach made noises.
I tiptoed to the closet and ate a
salami sandwich. But I had the wrong bag.
It was Jimmy's lunch.

"Ronald Morgan, is that you chewing?"
Miss Tyler asked.
All the children looked at me.
And Jimmy cried because he didn't
want my sandwich.

5

Then, when Alice was reading
—she's in the Mariners—
my group had to do a workbook page.
I didn't remember how to do it
so I asked Rosemary.
"Don't you even know how to do that?"
Rosemary asked.
And she's in the dumb group,
just like me.

After I finished the workbook page,
I wrote my initials on the thirsty sheet
and went into the hall for a drink of water.
Mrs. Gallop's third-grade class was having recess,
and I stood in line with them.
"Hi, Johnny," I said, and he said hi to me.

He showed me how to hold my finger
over the faucet.
Some of the water landed on the floor.
Most of it landed on Joy Farley's dress.

Mrs. Gallop took me to Miss Tyler
and said, "Ronald Morgan may never
get to third grade if he doesn't learn
to behave himself."
And I heard Rosemary say, "Ronald Morgan
may never get to third grade anyway.
He still can't read."

During recess we went outside to play ball.
I played left field because I don't
catch very well.
Only one ball came near me.
I ran for it.

I missed, and my ice cream money fell out of
my pocket.

"You just lost the game, Snakey," Billy yelled.

And Tom said, "What did you expect from that kid?"

When lunchtime came, I had no money
for ice cream.
I watched Jimmy eat my peanut butter sandwich.
He said he'd starve to death without it.
So all I had was half of Rosemary's candy bar
and one of Billy's cookies.

After lunch Miss Tyler called the Rockets
to the reading circle. I'm a Rocket.
Rosemary read the first sentence.
And Tom read the next one.
They didn't make any mistakes today.
When it was my turn,
I said, "Sally was a horse."
Miss Tyler said, "Ronald Morgan.
That's not right."
Rosemary said, "Sally *saw* a *house*."
And Tom said, "Some Rocket you are."

It was almost time to go home.
Miss Tyler said,
"I think the plant monitor has forgotten
to water the plants again."
Guess who the plant monitor is?

I got up and watered all the plants,
but while I was doing the last one,
the best one, I looked out the window.
Somehow I knocked the pot off the windowsill.

When it was finally time to go home,
Miss Tyler gave me a note.
"Ronald Morgan," she said.
"Take this note home.
Try to read it by yourself.
If you can't I'm sure your mother
will help you."

On the way home I read the note.

Dear Ronald,
  I'm sorry you had a
sad day.
  Tomorrow will be a
happy day because it's my
birthday.
  You and I will make it
happy.
          Love,
          Miss Tyler

Hey.

I read that whole note by myself.

I can read.

Wait till I tell Michael.

He's my best friend.

"Hello, Michael? This is Snakey.

Guess what?

I just found out I can read.

And guess what else?

It's Miss Tyler's birthday.

I think I'll bring her a plant.
I know she needs one."